Joshua's Dragon

Written by Stacey Glorioso
Illustrated by Katie Kelly

I am dedicating this book to all the Joshua's in the world. Despite the magnitude of obstacles standing in your way, your perseverance and determination to conquer your dragon and trudge on give all children the inspiration to conquer their own. To my cousin John, you will always be my hero!

Joshua's Dragon
Copyright © 2015 Stacey Glorioso
Illustrations Copyright © 2015 Katie Kelly
Hardcover ISBN: 9781616336882; 1616336889
Softcover ISBN: 9781616336899; 1616336897
eBook ISBN: 9781616336905; 1616336900

August 2015
Published in the United States of America

GUARDIAN ANGEL PUBLISHING, INC.
12430 Tesson Ferry Road #186
Saint Louis, Missouri 63128 USA
http://www.GuardianAngelPublishing.com

Joshua clenched his hands, waiting for the school bus to arrive. He was going on a field trip to the zoo.

And he was sure it would be loud. Joshua didn't like loud noises, but he was determined to go on the trip. He wanted to see a lion.

I know lions are the bravest animals in the world. So, I have to be brave, too.

Joshua settled
in a seat at the
front of the
school bus.

Children all around him babbled about baboons and pretended to be zoo animals. Soon, a faint wailing sound rippled from behind. HOWL! Joshua's body tensed when four more classmates chimed in. HOWL! HOWL!

I have to be brave, he thought.

He rummaged through his backpack to find his bubbles. But his hands were too sweaty. Joshua slumped in his seat and closed his eyes.

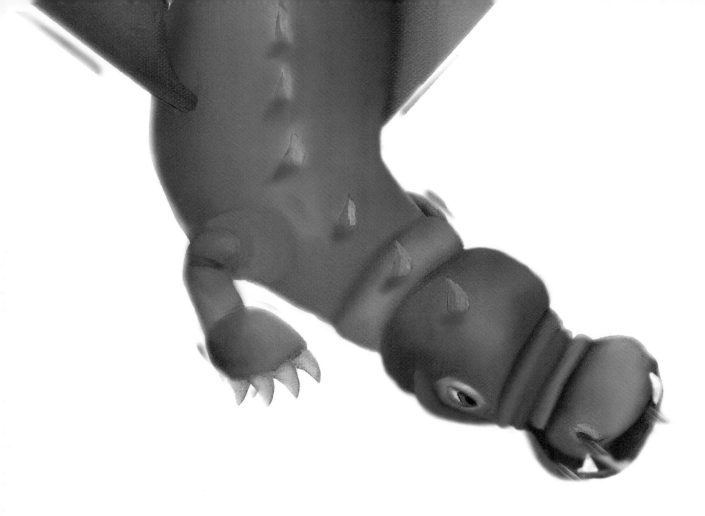

Joshua ran through the woods into a field. He spotted a large cave. "Maybe there's a lion in that cave."

But out from the cave soared a giant dragon!

"Go away, dragon!" yelled Joshua.

Instead, the dragon grinned. HOWL!

"Stop that!"Joshua stomped his foot.
"Scat!"
But the dragon's taunting grew louder.
HOWL! HOWL!

In a flash, Joshua took out his bubbles.

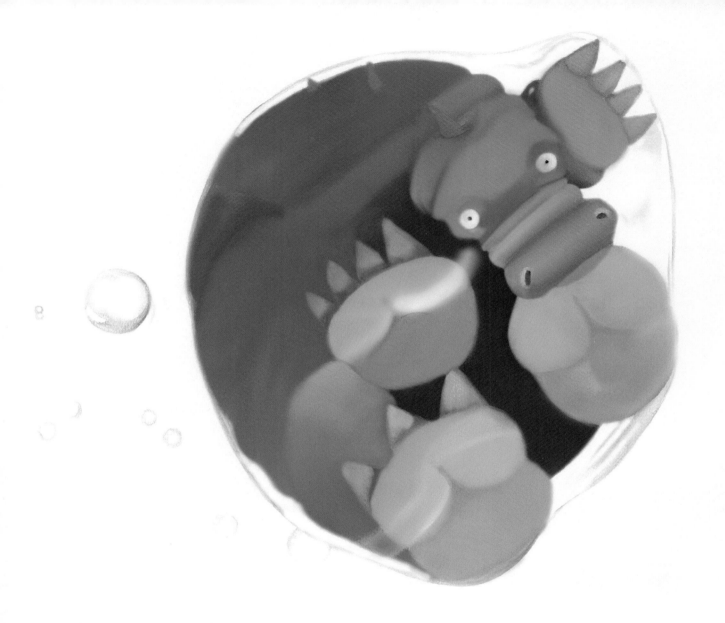

He blew and blew. Soon the dragon was trapped in a bubble! The noise stopped and the dragon floated away. Joshua howled like a wolf.

"Will we see the lions first?" he asked Mrs. Jane.

"No, the dolphin show is just about to begin," said Mrs. Jane.

Joshua's wide eyes lit up as the dolphin leaped from the water.

Then, the dolphin trainer took out a whistle. FEWWW!

Joshua stiffened his arms and clenched his jaw. I have to be brave, he thought.

He reached in his pocket to find his chewing gum. But his hands trembled.

He took a deep breath and closed his eyes.

Joshua sailed the ocean as
a sea captain on a dolphin.

Spotting palm trees,
he wondered if there's
a lion on that island.

But when he arrived, the dragon
was on the beach!
"It's you again!" shouted Joshua.
The dragon smirked and blew
a whistle. FEWW!

"Stop that noise!" Joshua
jumped up and down.
But the dragon huffed and puffed
harder. FEWW! FEWW!
Quickly, Joshua took out a piece of
chewing gum. He chewed and chomped
then squished his gum into the middle of
the dragon's whistle.
The noise stopped.

Joshua opened his eyes to watch the dolphin play. "Finally time to see the lions, Joshua," Mrs. Jane said.

Joshua's heart raced as a mighty lion climbed up a big rock. The lion stood tall, strong, and brave.

"Did you know lions are the bravest animals in the world?" he asked.

Then, the lion let out a powerful ear-piercing cry. ROAR! ROAR!

Joshua paced back and forth. The echo of the lion sent a shiver down his body. "I have to be brave," he thought. He put his headphones on with music.

But the lion's cry was like a fierce thunderstorm, rumbling around him.

Joshua closed his eyes again.

Joshua stood face-to-face with his dragon. "You silly dragon!" He shouted, "For once and for all, go away!"

The dragon squinted his eyes and grunted.
ROAR! ROAR!
Joshua took out his headphones again. "Hey, dragon."
He chuckled. "Would you like to hear some music?" He
placed his headphones on the dragon.

Joshua climbed up a rock. He stood tall, strong, and brave.

"The lion too loud for you, Joshua?" asked Mrs. Jane.

Joshua opened his eyes and smiled. "Don't worry about me, Mrs. Jane. I'm as brave as a lion! And when I close my eyes, I wish you could see what I see!"

So, Joshua leaped like a dolphin, roared like a lion, and gave Mrs. Jane a very loud hi-five.

CPSIA information can be obtained
at www.ICGtesting.com
Printed in the USA
LVIC04n0408221115
463574LV00006B/20